The Way to Captain Yankee's

written and illustrated by Anne Rockwell

Macmillan Publishing Company   New York
Maxwell Macmillan Canada   Toronto
Maxwell Macmillan International   New York   Oxford   Singapore   Sydney

For Mary Katherine and Jim

Macmillan Publishing Company is part of the Maxwell Communication
Group of Companies.
Macmillan Publishing Company, 866 Third Avenue, New York, NY 10022.
Maxwell Macmillan Canada, Inc., 1200 Eglinton Avenue East, Suite 200,
Don Mills, Ontario M3C 3N1.
First edition
Printed in the United States of America

10 9 8 7 6 5 4 3 2 1

The text of this book is set in 27 point Usherwood Medium.
The illustrations are rendered in silk screen on canvas with acrylics.

Library of Congress Cataloging-in-Publication Data
Rockwell, Anne F.
    The way to Captain Yankee's / written and illustrated by Anne Rockwell. — 1st ed.
        p.   cm.
    Summary: Miss Calico loses her way in going to visit Captain Yankee on
Pebble Point, but her map helps her find his house in the end.
    ISBN 0-02-777271-3
    [1. Maps—Fiction.] I. Title.
PZ7.R5943Wat   1994
[E]—dc20   92-44644

It was a beautiful morning
without a single cloud in the sky.
"Today I will visit Captain Yankee
in his new home on Pebble Point,"
Miss Calico said.

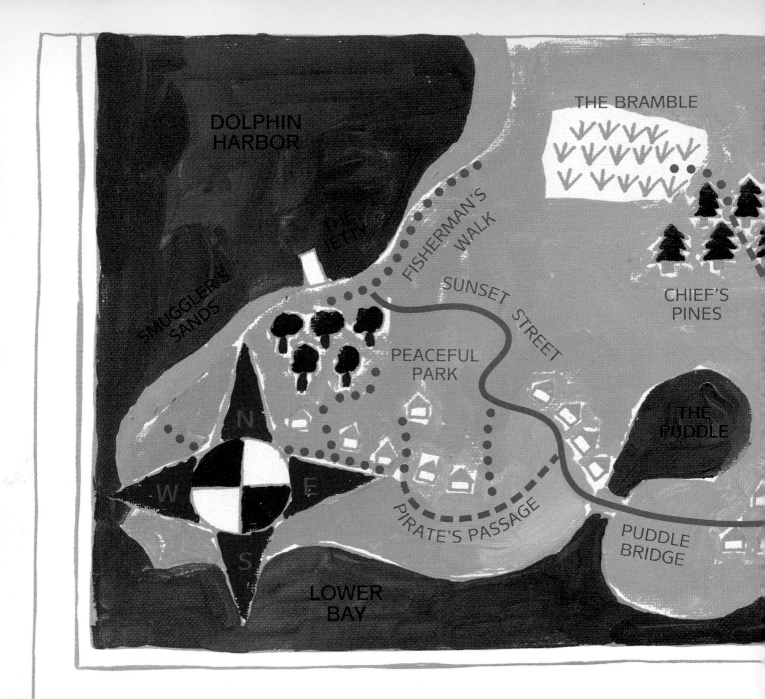

She looked at her map

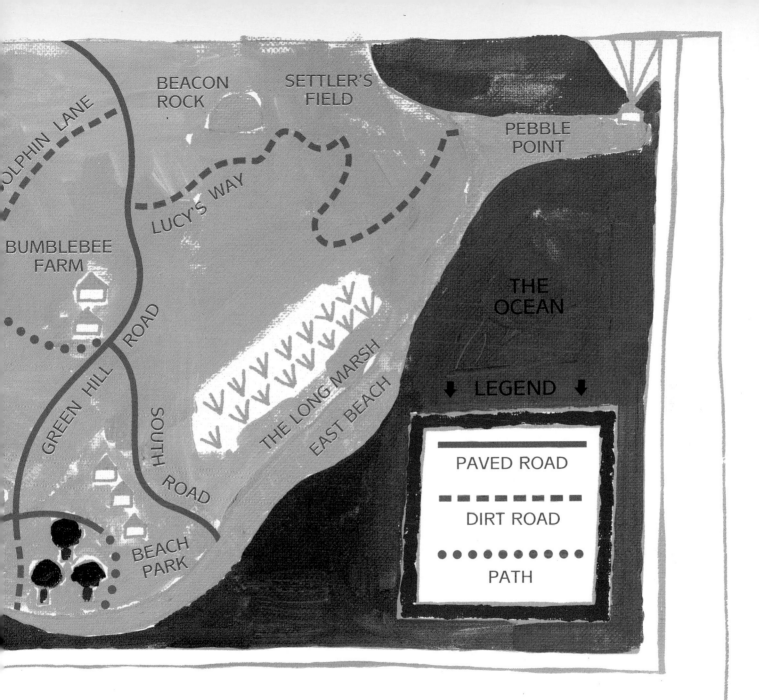

to see how to get there.

Then Miss Calico put on her straw hat,
put the map in her pocket,
and closed the door of
her little shingled house
at number four Pirate's Passage.
She went down Pirate's Passage
for three blocks,
until she came to Sunset Street.

She turned right on Sunset Street,
past the post office and Southwest Library.

She went over Puddle Bridge
and kept on going, right out of town.

When she came to the crossroad,
where Sunset Street crosses
Green Hill Road, she looked at her map.
Then she turned left on Green Hill Road.
Rambler roses and sweet peas
grew by the roadside.
Miss Calico picked some
for Captain Yankee.

She climbed up, up, up
Green Hill Road.

The sun was shining bright.
The road was steep.

Almost at the top of Green Hill,
across from South Road,
was Bumblebee Farm.
"Good morning," said Katie Potts.
"Would you like a glass of lemonade?"
"Indeed I would," said Miss Calico.
She stopped and bought some
lemonade to drink, and a jar of honey
to take to Captain Yankee.

From the top of the hill
Miss Calico could see the wide blue sea.
She watched a schooner sailing away
while she walked along the road.

She thought of how happy she would be
when she saw her friend Captain Yankee again.
She had not seen him for a long, long time.

Miss Calico got so interested in
watching the schooner grow smaller
and smaller as it sailed away,
she walked past Lucy's Way.

Instead, Miss Calico
turned left at Dolphin Lane.
The sign on the rock
was covered with weeds,
so she couldn't read what it said.

She walked and walked,
through a place where pine trees grew.
Miss Calico liked the way the hot sun
made the pine needles smell.
But soon Dolphin Lane was not
a road anymore.
It was just a path
leading out of the forest.

Soon it was not even a path.
She had walked into
a big, huge blackberry bramble
that was all scratchy and thorny.
None of the berries were ripe,
and poor Miss Calico had lost her way
to Captain Yankee's.
But suddenly she said,
"It's a good thing I brought my map!"

She took the map out of her pocket
to look at it again.
She saw that
Dolphin Lane did go
through a forest, turn into a path,

DOLPHIN HARBOR

THE BRAMBLE

THE JETTY

FISHERMAN'S WALK

SMUGGLER'S SANDS

PIRATE'S PASS

and end at the bramble.
She also saw that she had walked
past Lucy's Way,
quite some distance back.

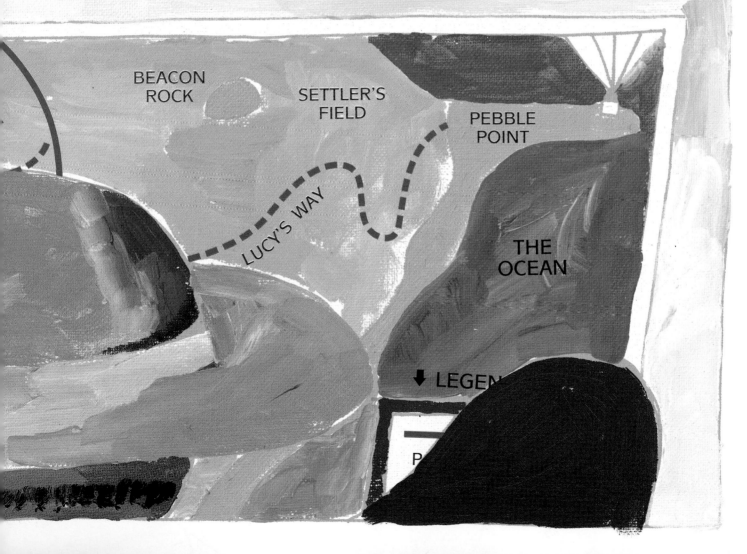

So Miss Calico
had to turn around and go back
in the direction she had come.
Back she went down Green Hill Road.
She found the break
in the wall
that led to the road
called Lucy's Way.

It was an old dirt road,
just as the map had said.
It twisted and turned, went uphill and down,
past Beacon Rock and Settler's Field.

PEBBLE
POINT

Finally Lucy's Way ended
at the top of a cliff by the sea.
Rickety steps led down to the shore.
A sign said PEBBLE POINT.

Miss Calico went carefully
down the rickety steps,
out to a little rocky spit of land

surrounded by waves of sparkling sea.
At the end of the spit a lighthouse stood
all bright and freshly painted.

And there was Captain Yankee.
He said, "I'm mighty glad
to see you, my friend.
You're just in time for lunch!"